W9-BUC-915

Cozy Light, Cozy Night

By Elisa Kleven

Creston Books

Autumn

R0440036825

Earth is turning, sun is up, cocoa's cozy in a cup.

Cozy toes in fuzzy boots, cozy pits in purple fruits,

Crunchy leaves beneath our feet, a snappy, crackly, cozy beat.

Cozy trees in red and yellow, cardinal's a cozy fellow.
Pumpkins shine in viney rows, breezes soft as oboes blow.

Nuts are cozy in their shells,

Clapper's cozy in its bell,

Bells ring, cozy in a tower

We sing, cozy in a shower.

Cozy apples wrapped in dough,

Crust above and crust below.

Cozy sweater, cozy pants,

Banjo music, jump and dance.

Winter

Cozy smell of sizzling cakes, drizzles turning into flakes.

Softly falling snow crochets a coverlet of lace,

Turns an empty lot into a cushioned, cozy place.

Padded jumps and fluffy falls,

Clumps of powder, packed in balls,

Cozy, frozen family

Dressed in mittens, caps, and shawls.

Cozy bread in braided loaves, toasty stockings by the stove,

Popcorn skitters, puffs and pops, cozy bottoms, cozy tops.

Candles sparkle, colors stream, cozy pictures light our dreams,

Crocodiles and kangaroos in coats of snowy cream.

Spring

Speckled eggs in cozy nests, cozy legs in Sunday best.

Bugs are cozy in their flowers, branches cozy, twined in bowers.

Picture's cozy in a locket, keys clink, cozy in a pocket.

Puppies in a crazy chase,

Romp and frolic, roll and race,

Tumble in a cozy jumble,

Lick a baseball player's face.

Cozy monarch butterflies, a ripple of orange wings,

Cozy ballerinas pirouette on jiggly strings.

Cozy matzo balls in soup, cozy pasta in a loop,

Cozy baby sleeping on a sunny springtime stoop.

Summer

Cozy sunhats, stitched and sewn, ice cream's cozy in a cone.

Cozy moss on tangled roots, cozy sand and swimming suits.

Cozy sound of carousel, a crazy quilt of notes,

Cozy little rocking waves, cozy bobbing boats.

Starfish snuggle, cozy in their salty, swaying pools,
Beach glass polka dots the sand, ocean-polished jewels.

Long and cozy shadows holding hands in lemon light,

Cozy flocks of pelicans and sandpipers in flight.

Milky moon shines, bright and high,

Earth twirls, tucked into the sky,

Stars swirl, blue and green and white,

Cozy light and cozy night.

Elisa Kleven is the author and/or illustrator of over 30 picture books. Favorites with children and adults alike, Elisa's books have received awards and honors from the American Library Association, The New York Times, The Junior Library Guild, School Library Journal, and the American Institute of Graphic Arts. Her pictures from *Abuela* are part of a traveling show organized by the Minnesota Children's Museum, and her story *The Paper Princess* has been adapted for two theater productions, one in Ireland and the other in California. Elisa lives in the San Francisco Bay Area with her family and pets. To learn more about Elisa and her books, visit her web site: www.elisakleven.com